THE FURRY CITIZENS

YOU WILL FALL IN LOVE WITH THEM...

Written and Illustrated by Rita Parekh

Rita S. Parekh

Qurate
quratebooks.com

THE FURRY CITIZENS

You Will Fall In Love With Them

Rita S. Parekh

Published in 2025

© Published by

Qurate Books Pvt. Ltd.
Goa 403523, India
www.quratebooks.com
Tel: 1800-210-6527, Email: info@quratebooks.com

ISBN: 978-93-58989-90-8

Disclaimer

Reasonable care and cautions have been taken to avoid errors and omissions in this publication, they have crept in inadvertently. This publication has been sold on the terms and conditions and with understanding with the author, publisher, printers and sellers should not be liable in any manner for any inconvenience, damage and loss caused to anyone by the errors and omissions of this book.

The characters may be fictional or based on real events, but in any case, it doesn't spread any negativity towards religion, language and caste. In case plagiarism is detected neither the compiler nor the publisher is responsible. Author should be solely responsible for their contents.

Preface

This is a sentimental, humorous, and action-packed story revolving around a beautiful kind but strong-willed young Indian girl Netra and the 27 street animals (Dogs and Cats) one of which is a pet of an affluent family.

Humans helping furry citizens and later furry citizens helping humans, an amazing interaction that endlessly entertains children as well as adult animal lovers. It also puts across the much-needed message to those who are intolerant towards the other life forms.

It is just a matter of realization and this realization comes to one in any form at any point of time in one's life and it changes the way one looks at life forever. This realization happened to Netra. Never in her dreams had she thought that she would feel for these street animals so much and would stand up for them so strongly. There was a time when Netra herself was so scared of dogs…..

Acknowledgement

I dedicate this book to all the animal lovers, sympathizers and care takers in India and the world over who relentlessly and selflessly work for their cause and are the reason for the existence of compassion, positivity and humanity on this planet. I know how difficult the task is. My big salute to all the animal caretakers and feeders. They have been my constant inspiration.

Furthermore, I profoundly thank and dedicate this book to my husband Late Shree Sunil Parekh who has constantly been the tower of my strength for whatever I have been able to do for the worthy causes.

Lots of love, happiness and blessings to all the animals, birds and other life forms the world over.

Contents

Disclaimer 3

Preface...5

Acknowledgement 7

An Honour Bestowed So Rightfully.....................11

It was not a long time ago...................................14

The first interaction..18

A whole new world unfathomed amidst
such hustle and bustle..23

A complete shift in situation..... 38

In the face of a fresh new challenge......................49

The venture was full of action and fun.................56

Emotions, Smiles, and Celebrations.... 72

An Honour Bestowed So Rightfully.....

Netra opened her eyes to a perfect day. Gazing through the window she smiled to herself in wonderment. Everything seemed so unbelievable. The last few years had completely changed her life. She was introduced to a whole new world that was always there around her but she hadn't perceived it so far. Though best in whatever she did, she carried no weight on her back of any serious goals to be accomplished. But now she had one and that was to fill their hard lives with love, care, and happiness.

Today was a significant day. A momentous event was waiting for them all. Mr. Gautam zealously hurried through his routine as he wanted to reach the venue before time. Mama and Raghunath were overexcited and had taken over the responsibility of conveying all 27 of them to the location on time.

The most awaited moments finally arrived. Netra's eyes sparkled as she spoke addressing a warm and enthusiastic crowd. "No words can express my feelings at this instance."

"It is indeed a proud moment for us all." She continued… Netra was so overwhelmed with emotions that tears of joy popped out into her eyes intermittently.

"I thank you all my dear children for being such an important part of my life and for showering my heart with your immense selfless love. I on behalf of everyone here would like to express the most sincere gratitude towards The Furry Citizens. They have proved once again that they are the man's best buddies and that they are second to none."

"Honestly, you all are the most wonderful and the most responsible citizens of this planet. And maybe this one thing that we humans need to learn from you all non-human citizens is the never-ending, selfless and unconditional love that you all forever radiate."

"I feel blessed and honoured today."

"Finally but importantly I would like to take an opportunity to thank all the beautiful people sitting out there in the front row for serving as the animal injustice warriors and helping me sail through the struggle for the cause of these innocent beings."

Following this short oral expression from Netra, amidst a huge round of applause, all 27 of them were taken onto the stage and honoured with the highest national award for showing their extraordinary bravery and humanity towards the human race thereby recognizing the special relationship between animals and humans...

***

It was not a long time ago.....

Netra was a young benevolent soft-spoken girl. Despite being compassionate and proximal to nature, she was afraid of any close interaction with the animals.

But once while she was going to college, she noticed two jittery, shivery, skinny dogs hiding under a parked private bus just a few meters away from her apartment. Netra felt a pang of discomfort at the sight initially but within seconds it got converted into a deep sympathy. She clumsily parked her car parallel to the potted plants that lined up the edge of the busy road and hastened across with a packet of biscuits that she had in her bag. Standing a few yards away, she fearfully bowed down and quickly kept a few rectangles in front of the dogs looking into their sunken dispassionate eyes. Surprisingly the biscuits disappeared as quickly as they were kept, into those ravenously hungry stomachs. Netra experienced a sense of gratification and happiness as never before, as she drove down to her destination. This happiness never ceased to exist but it continued as a sacred ritual. However, it was never a mere routine for Netra but something that had begun to define her.

***

The first interaction....

Quite incidentally, while feeding the duo skinny dogs, Netra would see a few other dogs staring hopefully from the other side of the road. As now her fear was on the decline and fondness on the incline, she went towards the dogs hoping to give them some food. But the dogs ran inside a huge dilapidated gate that seemed unguarded. Hesitatingly, Netra tried to peep through the half-open gate. What she saw inside was a huge unruly open space; on one side of which stood a big structure made of metal sheets painted in blue with a couple of trucks lined up. Suddenly an old guard, maybe in his seventies came out and enquired with Netra, "Yes madam, how can I help you?"

"No....I see a few dogs here staring at me every day when I feed the dogs across. Sooo... maybe I thought if you don't mind, I would like to give them some food," said Netra.

Hearing this, the old guard was overjoyed. "Definitely madam, definitely," he remarked.

And without wasting any time, he called out a few names. In the blink of an eye, a whole lot of almost 20-25 dogs came rushing from all directions. The scene that greeted Netra's eyes was awesome and breathtaking. Never before in her life had she seen so many dogs rushing towards her, wagging their tails happily. The dogs stopped a few meters away in bewilderment.

"Behave and thank this madam. She has got food for you all." He spoke to the dogs as if they were his babies.

The old guard Mama, like people who called out to him there, took the biscuits and the dog food from Netra's hands and instructed another young guard to spread it out on a plastic sheet a few steps away. To her dismay, the dogs just wildly pounced upon the food, each one of them trying to get a lion's share.

That night Netra simply kept thinking about the dogs. "Really how hungry they must be," she whispered to herself.

Something had got triggered within her invariably. The next day she rolled up a few extra chapattis, grabbed a few packets of biscuits and some dog food, and went to feed the dogs at the compound. It became a regular feature gradually. Also, the dogs would wait eagerly near the gate looking out for Netra. However, fortuitously if she wouldn't turn up a particular day, slowly losing hope they would slip away in some cozy corners.

***

A whole new world unfathomed amidst such hustle and bustle....

These 25 dogs in the compound seemed rugged, unrefined, tough, and intimidating but when Netra had a close peep into their lives, it told a completely different story. Their lives were miserable. As the days passed, Netra grew emotionally attached to them and so were the dogs. There were two cats Simba and Vini as well in the compound who would sit at a distance and wait for their turn on food, coupled with a few pats from Netra. However, the felines were often seen

lazy
Ladoo.

romping around with Chirag and Browny. The generous old guard Mama was heartily fond of the dogs in the compound and had named them all, in his special way. Moreover, each one of them wore a unique trait and followed a particular behavioural pattern.

Like LALU, a huge strongly built white dog, leader of the whole lot, had all the leadership qualities. Mammoth was his conscious level and he was so loving, responsive, and intelligent that sometimes you may forget that he is a dog. It took quite a while for Netra to earn a good friendship with LALU. Nevertheless, affection between the two was at another level later. Yes one more thing about LALU was he wouldn't eat anything thrown on the floor. Often other dogs offered him the signs of submission.

MY SOUL! A great female adult dog, who was on the verge of amputation while she was a pup, had a rod inserted in her right thigh. According to the doctor, it was either a miracle or someone's trust and love that had worked for her. Being very close to Netra's heart, she called her MY SOUL. Both shared an exceptional bond.

BHURA was also a dominant male dog. The iris of one of his eyes was noticeably lighter. Bhura was a flirtatious light brown dog often busy wooing the female dogs around. Lalu and Bhura wouldn't get along at all.

KALI an adult female dog often used to be jealous of My Soul, as Netra hugged and patted her a lot. Kali would always try to put her head in between and steal a few pats from Netra.

ELIYA was Kali's daughter, an active medium-sized black dog with white patches here and there, mostly seen playing with Mysoul.

SHAILA, AH! Such a playful dog. He ate heartily and there was always a basic invitation to play on his face.

CHIRAG was a black hairy mix breed dog. It did not belong to the compound like other dogs but had sought refuge there once while it was a pup. Once on a rainy drainy night the old guard Mama had seen him outside the gate all alone, scared and wet, and had taken him inside. An all-time favorite of Mama, he would always sit near his feet. He very well got along with all the other dogs but preferred to eat quietly away from others. Maybe it was his way of respecting the brigade he didn't belong to from birth.

BROWNY, a young male dog with intermittent light and dark brown patches kept to himself. Happy in his own space, he was always found with some piece of paper or rug hanging from his mouth.

Smaller dogs have to display in attitude what they lack in size and CHHOTU was living proof. PARI was a super sweet girl. TOBU and JAGGU were affectionate and gentle. RESHU was alert but fearful and skeptical. NANI, the eldest was sensible, protective, and responsible. LADOO liked lounging around and sleeping more than running and playing. His hobby included eating and doing nothing. TESSA on the other hand was over-reactive and dramatic. LOLA, MONU, ROCKY, TOMMY, RUM, LISA, BUDDY, OREO…all of them were fabulous and adorable.

Seeing Netra they would come all over her wagging their tails. Lalu would pull her down and try to tuck his husky burly body into Netra's lap.

Mysoul would come limping and start licking Netra with deep affection.

Covetous Kali would do everything possible to draw Netra's attention from Mysoul towards her and acquire some warm hugs.

Browny would run in circles with joy.

Shaila would come running as fast as he could and sometimes move past Netra in excitement.

Tessa would stand up on her hind legs and Jaggu would roll on the ground.

Nani, the oldest would give them all her special intimidating look for the ungovernable and chaotic behaviour.

Mau Mau the snowy white, furry, stylish pet cat of an affluent family residing in the neighborhood would sit on her balcony and hiss, meow, purr, chirp, chat, howl, and yowl the whole day long at everyone in the compound. Besides modish apparel and trendy collars, she also wore scads of Cattitude. All the furies were friends with her but Chirag had a special liking for her.

Mau Mau's pawrents had recently adopted a 4 month old pup Sky. Mau Mau openly showed her displeasure at home coming of this new member in the form of her sibling. Sky was over energetic and somewhat unruly in his ways. Mau Mau shunned him for his uncultured behaviour. She wouldn't mind him as far as he minded his own business but would hiss at him and even slap him in rapid succession when he excitedly chased her.

Hysterically greeting familiar as well as unfamiliar people and devouring anything and everything at hand was Sky's passionate habit. However he was extremely pretty and adorable and everybody around just loved him.

It was the happiest moment for all of them whenever Netra was around. Over time Netra trained them all about food civility by making sure there was no competition for food. Now there was no food aggression and snapping at each other. Contrarily they would wait until Netra gestured them to eat. Over the next two years, Netra had many more mouths to feed. She also neutered and vaccinated them all. To match with the expenditure, she had taken up the teaching job to create an extra source of income.

Furthermore, there were some labourer's hutments towards the end of the compound. Seeing Netra feed the dogs these labourers' children too would share their food with dogs from whatever little they had. As a gesture of admiration Netra would distribute some chocolates to them occasionally. It was always the happiest moment for Netra when she was amidst the dogs, children, and the security guard Mama.

***

A complete shift in situation.....

In reality, this huge plot which was home to the 25 street dogs was bought by Mr. Karodimal a well-known builder and a bigwig. The work had not yet started as the plot was trapped in the web of legalities. He therefore presently used it as a small cement unit for his other upcoming complexes. Now after things got sorted out and as the construction work was about to start, there was a complete shift in the situation. The site Manager who was appointed was inconsiderate and rude.

"Madam you are not allowed to enter this premises," he said bluntly once when he saw Netra inside the compound.

"But I have been feeding these dogs for long and they don't have any other source of food here inside," Netra replied in a polite but firm tone.

"That is no concern to us." He continued roughly.

In a fit of rage, he called out to Mama and started threatening him. Mama and Netra exchanged a brief look in despair. Mama tried to comfort Netra as much as he could nonverbally with his reassuring facial expression. Though Netra was shattered and almost in tears. She was extremely worried for the dogs. Mama respected Netra immensely and disapproved of anyone speaking discourteously to her. He, therefore, called up Netra and asked her to leave a bag of dog food with him and that he would quietly feed them all when no one was around. The comforting and reassuring words of Mama came as a great relief for Netra but it didn't

last long. Soon Mama was removed and the whole security changed. All the hell broke loose on NETRA. Now there was no one to look after the dogs inside. News that the site manager had given security, orders to remove the dogs by any means added to Netra's predicament. But by the grace of God, the security and some labourers staying inside denied obeying the orders. Netra pleaded and explained to the manager Ghorpade that the dogs would slowly adjust themselves around by the time the complex came up. She also made him aware of the law of the land that stated: dislocation of animals was a punishable offense. Nonetheless, it all fell on the deaf ears.

Netra now fed the dogs at six in the morning and the people inside supported her. But the time had to go the adverse way. Netra met with a really bad accident and got immobilized due to a fracture. In front of the X-ray machine, tears rolled down Netra's cheeks, thinking about the dogs.

Two days had passed since dogs were on their own without any food or water.

Nor they had Mama with them neither they had seen Netra. The place had lost its usual friendly and welcoming atmosphere. It looked like all the furry souls were down in the dumps and the unhappiness had forever settled on their faces. The otherwise playful Shaila was listless. Browny had settled on a heap of sand with his tail tucked in. Resting the head on his forehands and the tail hanging with intermittent slow wags, Eliya had balanced herself on a pipe. Mysoul and Kali who usually played cat and mouse sat abreast holding their heads low. Bhura had gone hangry and was trying to intimidate every passer-by. Lalu too had worn a long face albeit he was quite calm and composed. Seeing her friends in such condition Mau Mau too turned dull and cheerless and hardly ate which made her pawrents wonder. Though unawares Sky was his usual ways.

Suddenly with a small creak, two men pushed themselves inside the premises keeping the door ajar. Their faces were spiteful, threatening, and suggestive. Glancing around the poorly lit vacant lot, the duo hurriedly arranged some food on the floor. And the next moment, wearing a false smile they started calling upon the dogs to feast on it.

The sight and the smell almost lured the starving dogs. They lifted their heads with an irresistible impulse to eat. The men were endeavouring to tempt the dogs into their complot. However, the dogs had seen through their malicious intentions and were suspiciously glaring at the men.

In-between, unable to curb the hunger pangs, Browny and Vini slowly advanced towards the food. But Lalu right away showed his annoyance with a short sharp bark. Nani the elderly dog too warned Browny to stay away from the food with her soft growl and stern face.

Browny with a sheepish grin, avoiding any eye contact backed off. Cowering and hunching, Vini the cat too sprang back onto the wall and sat beside the angrily staring diligent and wise Simba. Mau Mau was staring at her as well from her balcony. The duos were radiating guilt. Eventually, the men had to leave with their tasks unfinished.

Few more days passed and Netra grew anxious and worried at the mere thought of dogs going hungry with no source of food at all. She sent her younger brother to seek help from the security personnel there but they were afraid as it would risk their job.

Meanwhile Raghunath a cement truck driver came over and offered to help. He would then pick up the food from Netra's house and smuggle it inside at night. The construction workers and their children too assisted Raghunath in this task. Lalu the pack leader ensured that everyone ate quietly. But Shaila, Browny, Blacky, and Tessa unable to hold back their extreme, exhilarating joy would often resort to excited barking, playful attacks, and vigorous wagging of tails at the sight of food. Howbeit, at the brief sight of Lalu's wrinkled nose, stiff-legged stance, and raised bristled tail vibrating from side to side both would tuck their tails and start eating orderly. Mau Mau would glance at the dogs eating, from the corner of her window, and feeling satisfied would happily go to sleep. Netra was quite relieved due to Raghunath's help but she knew it wasn't the real solution.

In the meantime, Netra was visited by one Mr. Gautam a journalist and an ardent animal lover who resided in the vicinity. He came as a great help and support to Netra throughout the struggle. He spoke and tried to convince people at key positions in the builder's office but all in vain.

As a last resort, Mr. Gautam and Netra consulted an animal welfare officer and requested him to intervene. Mr. Charania was a renowned officer. He called upon the project manager to demand a written explanatory report regarding the complaint lodged by Netra within 72 hours.

To submit a convincing report the project manager Ghorpade resorted to a plan which was a complete eyewash. He simply sent his men for a photo op with the dogs to showcase that they were taking care of the dogs thus dismissing all the reasons for permitting Netra inside the premises. Nevertheless, the dogs were too smart to be bullied. They would come close to the food but smartly miss the click. With the efforts not paying up the men got frustrated and left the place. Mr. Charania exhibited a proactive approach and constituted an honest investigative report. Finally, the builder's office being unable to provide a satisfactory reply was sent a notice by the National Animal Welfare Board.

Not wanting to get trapped into any further legal web, the builder's office gave Netra permission to feed and look after the dogs.

It was truly a euphoric moment for Netra as well as Mr. Gautam who had been a backbone support system throughout her struggle. And the day Netra met the dogs again after a long duration of her bed rest; the furry souls were over whelmed. It all went on well for days to come without any conflict whatsoever. Even Mama dropped in occasionally to meet them all.

Meanwhile, Mr. Karodimal's 10-year-old grandson had also grown to like these furry souls at the compound. He would almost regularly stop by to play with them in the afternoon while returning from school. He had even palled up with Netra as it was also the same time when Netra came to feed the dogs. Everything was so hunky-dory at the place with the feeling of overwhelming affection in the air.

***

In the face of a fresh new challenge.....

One afternoon after spending sometime happily playing with the dogs when Yohan was about to alight his car parked a few yards away from the gate, an untoward incident occurred. Three men appeared out of the blue, toppled a gunny bag over Yohan, thrust him into the van that was kept ready behind Yohan's car, and in a blink of an eye abducted him.

It would have gone completely unnoticed if Mau Mau whiling away her time in the balcony wouldn't have been vigilant plus Haldi and Coco resting under the parked vehicle across the road wouldn't have been watchful. Both the dogs instantly leaped to their feet and went crazy with rapid barking. Hearing them the pack inside the compound too flew up rushing out through the gate and started barking as though they had been alerted to an unusual occurrence in the area.

Yohan's chauffeur, who was dozing off in the car, woke up oblivious to the entire episode. Amidst these vocal cues, Netra spotted the driver peeping through the gate as if trying to locate Yohan.

"Rameshji, where is Yohan?" Netra called out to the driver. But he seemed clueless. "Did you not see him?"

"He just came out of the gate a couple of minutes ago." She continued anxiously.

Netra had sensed that something was amiss and it was concerning Yohan. Dogs were still barking frantically as if conveying something. Everyone at the sight started searching for Yohan but he was nowhere to be seen. Finally, the security-in-charge called up at Yohan's residence, and later the police were informed.

The next 24 hours were hard on everyone. The most alarmed and perturbed were the dogs. They were the only ones who knew what tragedy had befallen Yohan. Netra divulged this to the police but they just disregarded it.

The police enquired with everyone in and out of the vacant plot, interrogated every potential suspect, and investigated various probable aspects. But the exploration was leading them nowhere. Mr. Karodimal was a well-known builder and so the news spread across the masses like a wildfire. This created a lot of media pressure on the police department to nab the culprits at the earliest and put them behind bars. Also, time was crucial as Yohan was vulnerable and his life was in grave danger. Yohan's family was in intense shock. Police were vigilant but the kidnappers showed no stir at all. With not a single ransom call, the investigators had to settle for revenge as a cause of the kidnap. However, police had very little to work on and there was still nothing conclusive of the crime.

A few days later one quiet afternoon when Netra was feeding the dogs she felt as if Haldi and Coco communicated something vocally from outside of the boundary wall. The very next moment all the dogs dashed through the open gate and started yelping and yowling. When Netra ran out on the street to see what was happening, she saw Haldi growling and thrashing its tail while coco snarling and clutching onto a person's shirt. He was one of the heavy equipment operators at the site. Netra fleetly sprinted across the road and only after a struggle could pull Coco off the man. Initially, she stood shocked in disbelief as Coco had never behaved so belligerently. On contrary, he was the most amicable and docile little creature. But subsequently, it started making sense and she right away confided in the police.

Inspector Sharad More detected a hint of sincerity in Netra's voice. He rather sensed the veracity of the indication given out by the dogs and decided to go along with it. So he formed a squad that also included the K9 police dog, Brutus. Brutus was a five-and-a-half-year-old German Shepherd and an efficient scent discrimination trailing dog. He had a characteristic springy gait and proud manner of carrying itself. Being a passive alert dog, who, unlike an aggressive one, would just sit and stare at the location of the scent, made him perfectly suitable for such a sensitive task.

Netra took the help of a few labourers' children and managed to get the suspect's shirt as a reference for Brutus. However, Brutus was also brought into the crime scene once by his handler so that it could sniff out the perpetrator. The Lalu Brigade was happily amazed to see Brutus at the compound but out of admiration when they greeted Brutus, the latter just ignored them all.

Since the dogs had been playing an extensive role in this case right from the beginning, the mission was named "Mission Furry Friends."

***

The venture was full of action and fun.....

Inspector More and his team were all set to leave for the mission the very next morning.

However making the first move, the canine buddies at the compound, along with Haldi and Coco set out to hunt for Yohan in the wee hours already. Abandoning the differences, they had all pitched in for the common undertaking. Even Lalu and Bhura, who never got along, pulled their efforts together. Mau Mau stole away from her house to join the gang. Sky too slipped out behind Mau Mau covertly and stealthily unnoticed. Simba and Vini too were in to lend a hand.

Determining the directionality of the trail the furry citizens tracked along the route. All 27 of them were surrounded by the silent night. They marched ahead taking heed to the tiniest hints dropped in by the other street dogs at various locations. Lalu strode ahead. Simba and Vini ran intermittently to catch the pace. Bhura walked in with a swagger. Chhotu bounced boastfully. Almost everyone else marched behind. Playful Shaila ambled a bit. Ladoo dawdled thanks to his roly-poly plumpish shape and Mau Mau panted thanks to her inactive luxurious life. When Chirag noticed Mau Mau overly exhausted he offered her a ride on his back which she happily accepted. Though for every jerky step, she would hit Chirag on his head with her claw retracted paw to make him aware of all the inconvenience caused to her. At intervals, Lalu would take up the role of a disciplinarian to keep each member of the pack together. Whatever may be their ways they all had strong determination on their face.

Finally, after almost three hours of painstaking efforts, they were standing a few yards away from an abandoned structure that seemed to be the source of a familiar scent. It was a three-floor deserted factory.

Another twenty minutes they just bide their time patiently, weighing up the situation. Camouflaging themselves around the bushes they keenly observed the entire space for the signs of activity. Well-armed men were guarding the entrances. Dogs looked at each other with blank flabbergasted expressions. Certainly, it was something more to it. It was still an hour before dawn and consequently quite dark throughout.

Except for some yellow light sneaking out of a window on the second floor, the rest was partially illuminated by the dim moonlight peeping in through the surrounding bushes and trees. The team was in a bit of a conundrum. Before taking the plunge it was utterly important to have a quick look through the window. Everyone gazed hopefully at the spry little Vini. In a jiffy, she took up to the trunk. While hurrying through the large and small branches that followed, she slid her paw unsteadily on one of the slippery branches and almost toppled over. Cutting through the silence each one of them below reflexively yelped and sighed. Vini's pupils dilated and her heart almost skipped a beat. However, she managed herself. Holding on to a nearby branch and subsequently balancing herself on the edge of an adjoining bough she stretched enough to take the closest view possible through the window. Within minutes she was down amidst her buddies all bug-eyed, shocked and alarmed. Equally appalled was the team when it learned that Yohan was not the only one. There were many children set off in fear and trepidation.

Abruptly Mau Mau saw a glimpse of Sky trying to hide behind Ladoo. She got furious but Chirag calmed her down quickly reminding her of the crucial situation they were in. Though Mau Mau at the least warned Sky against any foolhardiness and asked him to stay safe.

Suddenly the rustling of leaves drew everyone's attention. Three men were found

conversing on the other side in a dark corner. Mysoul quickly slipped in there to spy on them. She broke in yet another piece of shocking news. All the children were going to be deported to some faraway place that very afternoon. The team communicated briefly. It was then decided that while Tessa and Lisa, the two drama queens would divert the attention of the men guarding at the entrance, half the team would take the opportunity and sulk inside. Things went on exactly as decided and in few minutes they were all inside the corridor. The rest waited in the wings. Haldi and Coco remained holed up in the bushes near the main gateway leading to the premises.

Once inside all of them spread across the area. Lalu and Bhura crept onto the second floor stealthily unnoticed. At the end of the corridor was a sturdy-looking man, guarding an equally sturdy metal door that perhaps had the children locked up inside. Lalu gestured to Simba the cat who he knew was following. Instantly picking up the command Simba swiftly leaped onto the parapet that ran parallel to the corridor, walked along until he reached its extremity, waited for a while, crouched low, sneaked, and pounced forcefully upon the guard's face, scratching him all over, giving him little chance to react. All bruised and battered the guard was so terrified that with a long voiceless scream he fell flat on the floor. Lalu and Bhura almost piercing their teeth through the guard's trousers pulled him aside so as not to be seen by anyone.

Both then cracked open the door with their head and peeped inside. The section of the hall that was visible revealed a ghastly scene. Children were sitting on the floor terrified, exhausted, and soiled, holding back their tears. Lalu was heartbroken at the sight. One of the abductors was sitting on a chair busy with his phone while the other patrolling across the room.

As Lalu and Bhura stood quietly contemplating the scene, they heard Mysoul and Kali softly growling from an anonymous location that was quite suggestive. They were seeking help. Lalu and Bhura breathed a sigh of relief when they saw Chirag, Mau Mau, and Buddy ducking through the parapet reaching out to Mysoul and Kali. Sneaking in behind the 3 was Sky. Lalu could see his tall standing, one brown and one white button ears jumping in air as he was moving behind Mau Mau which made him extremely anxious.

Suddenly an alerting meow emerged from Simba. One of the kidnappers who were guarding the children was approaching the doorway. The dogs backpedaled a few steps down the stairs. But the kidnapper's eyes quickly glanced through the corridor and disappeared inside.

They now knew that the only way was to barge into the room. Simba and Vini trotted through the half-closed window on the wall adjacent to the main door and alighted inside the room. At the same moment, Lalu and Bhura too just rushed in. As the cats suddenly pounced upon the men, weapons in their hands flung aside. They shrieked with a high-pitched sound in pain as the cats bit and scratched them all over. Next moment the dogs took over. They bit and dragged them to a corner. Seeing all his Furry Friends, Yohan's eyes sparkled. He emboldened all the children who were too shocked to understand what was happening. Yohan together with other children picked up the weapons and threw them off the window. One of the men tried to slip out but came across the sinewy Rocky in the doorway whose piercing gaze drew him back into the room.

On the third floor, Mysoul and Kali were waiting anxiously for help in a hideout a few steps away from the mysterious storeroom that was guarded by a man. They had an inkling that more children were hemmed in. Seeing Chirag, Mau Mau, and Buddy both gathered courage. But all of them were completely unaware that the mischievous little Sky had come along following them throughout. Suddenly from nowhere emerged Sky panting excitedly and happily wagging his tail, rushing towards the man in hope of some food. All of them were aghast at the scene. And the next moment they got worried for Sky's safety. Taking everyone by surprise, the unperturbed Mau Mau just walked to the man and started hissing at him. Seeing such a fearless confident dolled-up cat, the man was taken aback. Before he could figure out anything, the four dogs too came forward and firmly stood surrounding him. With scary growls and hisses, they chased the man off. Winning the trust and confidence of the children packed inside the storeroom, they let them off cautiously in small groups. Hearing the clamour of voices Tommy, Oreo, Lola, Tobby, Shaila, and few other dogs waiting downstairs too rushed up. Within few minutes it was sheer bedlam. Shaila in a hurry surged into the room adjacent to the hall on the second floor. The frisky little Vini followed him. As Shaila strained his eyes in the dull light trying to figure things out, he accidentally hit a music player lying there unattended. Startled, Vini just jumped high and a funny wig fell on her head. The duo got carried away by the tuneful music that flowed of the box and started playfully gambolling, jiggling, and joggling their bodies around. The noise drew Simba into the room.

Seeing Shaila and Vini irresponsibly dancing, Simba gave them both a grumpy Scowl. She bit Shaila's tail and growled at Vini. Shaila screamed in pain and Vini put off the wig. Both then submissively followed Simba. Mau Mau at the door too gestured and scowled at the duo as if saying, "How down market!" All the unruly hubbub and uproar compelled the kidnappers at the other ends to flee. But Ladoo, Chhotu, Jaggu, Reshu, Pari, and Nani were waiting down to welcome them with a scowl on their faces. The men stumbled and fell. Jaggu, Chhotu, and Reshu dragged them holding by their trousers and the hefty Ladoo rolled over them almost squashing the men against the ground. Reshu and Nani scared them out of their wits by barking at them fiercely.

By now it was dawn and inspector Sharad More along with his team reached the place. Netra, Mr. Karodimal, and Mau Mau's pawrents had also accompanied. Netra was extremely worried for all her canines and felines. Mau Mau and Sky being extremely pampered pets, their pawrents too were hugely anxious. Mr. Karodimal's eyes were desperately searching for Yohan. The whole place was in an uproar. Brutus too had reached the place with his handler. Coco and Haldi subtly communicated with Brutus. The police team ran up the flight of stairs and reached out to every corner of the factory. They arrested all the kidnappers and safely released all the children. Yohan too was one of them, whom a heavy machine operator working at the construction site had kidnapped due to some personal grudge against the builder Mr. Karodimal.

***

Emotions, Smiles, and Celebrations.....

Seeing Yohan safe and sound, Mr. Karodimal broke into tears. Brutus was in complete awe seeing the street wise street dogs operating aptly. When all the non-human citizens walked out successfully concluding the task, Brutus who once down regarded and ignored them all formally saluted each one of them. Spotting Netra, they all ran over to her. Few of them were barking and whining, whereas others were hanging their tongues out as if smiling. Some were holding their tails high whereas others wagging their tails so much that it wiggled their whole body. The whole episode had got Netra so emotional that she just gazed at all her furry babies with the fondest pride and joy. MauMau hopped cheerfully into her pawrent's arms followed by the exchange of a lot of hugs and kisses. And Sky over-excitedly ran in circles sometimes jumping back and forth mouthing, nipping and barking. It was the most gratifying moment for everyone.

The next few days were a reason to rejoice for so many agonizing families. It was a reason to celebrate for so many grieving pawrents. All the children were happily united with their loved ones. Netra had to call for a vet and spend quite a long time at the compound getting the entire furry baby's bruises and small wounds treated. However, the greatest impact of the entire event was on Mr. Karodimal. He had found a new fondness for the dogs and decided to give away a part of the land for building an animal shelter. Netra just went crazy with happiness hearing this and Mr. Gautam was happy as never before. Mama the old guard was put back on his job, this time especially to look after the dogs.

Regaining Mama gladdened the dogs. Also with the food provided by Netra, Raghunath the truck driver along with the labourer's children could now fearlessly feed them all.

After a couple of days, Netra and Mr. Gautam arranged for a small celebration for all the Furry Citizens at the compound. Brutus was invited as well. Mr. Karodimal too sent in presents with Yohan for the dogs as well as for the labourer's children with all the best wishes. All the dogs and the cats went crazy with so many delicious gourmet meals, treats, cakes, and a variety of toys to play with. Small water pools were also arranged, in which the dogs splashed water to their heart's content. MauMau and Sky too had come with their pawrents. Mau Mauate, played, and enjoyed with all her furry friends but with etiquette. Whereas Sky was insanely stimulated and was seen frolicking about the whole play area.

It is said that all's well that ends well. But this was not the end. Its happy consequences spread such that, it changed the perspective of the masses across towards the street animals, especially the dogs. The class of animal lovers increased many folds. And those who were intolerant towards them became accommodative.

One of the families of the rescued children took the initiative and the recommendation for the bravery award for the Furry citizens was sent to the concerned authority which was undisputedly accepted. Though this was just an acknowledgment of a beautiful bond between the human and the non-human citizens, in reality, this bond always existed and it will exist forever......

***